KEEP CALM
AND DO
BODMAS

Dear Thelma
With thanks
& Love
Nas ☺
xx

First published 2022

Published under licence by Brown Dog Books and
The Self-Publishing Partnership Ltd, 10b Greenway Farm, Bath Rd, Wick, nr. Bath BS30 5RL

www.selfpublishingpartnership.co.uk

ISBN printed book: 978-1-83952-465-3
ISBN e-book: 978-1-83952-466-0

Cover design by Kevin Rylands
Internal design by Andrew Easton
Illustrations by helixdesign.studio

Printed and bound in the UK

This book is printed on FSC® certified paper

KEEP CALM
AND DO
BODMAS

A LITTLE BOOK OF MEDITATION
TOOLS FOR TEENS

NASREEN PRITCHARD

For my
girls,
S and G
xx

What page is what?

It really is Go Shine!

My intention for this little book:

Firstly, hey! And thanks for checking this book out.

The idea for this book came years ago, and like a lot of ideas, they sit on the burner for a while.

Sometimes other things take priority and sometimes it's a case of 'just get on with it'.

However, I am a believer in 'there's a right time for everything' and so here we are now, 2021, and I've written it!

If you're reading this then you are likely to have lived through a school year or two like no other.

My intention for this book is to offer you a few tools to navigate the coming years with, but also some skills you can use for life.

I like maths! There, I've got it out of the way now!

I suppose maths makes sense to me as there are certain rules and formulas to follow, and if we learn and follow these, we are likely to get to the correct answer. I'm not saying I found maths easy, far from it ... I had a good teacher, which really is a huge start, and I enjoyed problem solving so I didn't mind working hard at it.

I mostly liked that there were certain *orders* to do things in.

Hence

BODMAS: The order you do things in.

So, using a mathematical analogy to order some meditation tools, to me, made sense ... I hope it will for you too!

I would like you to keep in mind as you read through this book that this is a journey and you're the passenger!

You've paid the ticket (price of the book) to get somewhere. There is no 'right' destination - YOU pick where you go, what YOU see and how long it takes to get there ... In fact, it may be better to say that you are the driver!

My wish is that this little book, can be a reminder for YOU, to be there for YOU, to take care of YOU!

As Dr Seuss says himself:

'There is no one alive, who is Youer than You.'

I hope you enjoy the journey!

BODMAS

It's just the order you do things in!

BODMAS BREAKDOWN

B.reathe

Definition: To take air into the lungs and then expel it.

I could play this two ways: tell you all the benefits of a breathing practice, or, share with you some of the things that became 'lightbulb' moments for me and let you have your own.

Firstly, breathing practice? Surely we breathe in and out and we don't need to practise that?
Yes, that's true, breathing is continuous and involuntary - it's automatic!
The respiratory system has that covered.

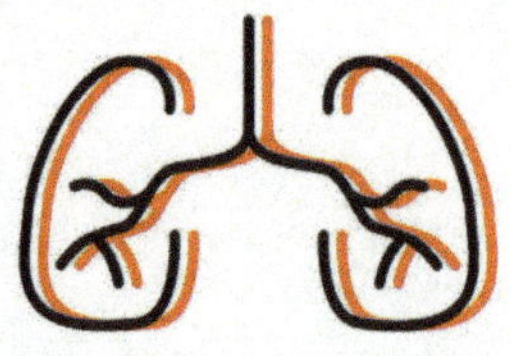

However, it is a feature of our body that is involuntary AND voluntary!

That's why we can take a deep breath and dive into a swimming pool without swallowing lots of water. It's also why, when we laugh hysterically, we sometimes say 'Stop, I can't breathe,' and we consciously try to connect with our breath again.

When I started to 'practise' breathing, I thought it was about getting better at it, and in a way that's true – like when we go for a run and we get out of breath, with 'practice' our breathing function 'gets better' and we can run for longer.

I learned, though, that the more I practised BREATH, the more it became like a friend - a friend that was always there, literally, even when I slept. It was always hanging around!

Remember, like our real-life friends, we want the best for them. We don't judge or put lots of expectations on them and when they are happy we can share in that happiness.

My wish for you is that you get real friendly with your breath!

BODMAS Practical Tools:

Use any of the breathing shapes shown in Chapter: Breathing Practices.

Going back to the definition of breathing, of course a full breath cycle is an inhale AND exhale. The IN so we can fuel, nourish and repair, and the OUT to release toxins and tensions, both physical and emotional. The balance of these two is the key for good function and harmony in the body. Good breathing techniques not only help us to have healthy bodies but healthy minds too. It can mean our concentration is better, our sleep is better and our decision making is better.

The techniques I have shared are just a selection to start with, so enjoy them, but explore others and find ones that you really love!

'Deep breaths are like little love notes to yourself.'

O.bserve

Definition: Simply put, OBSERVATION is the act of noticing.

Now, typically, or at least most commonly, the first way to observe/notice things may be with our eyes.

However, we have so many more tools to observe – our five senses: seeing, hearing, smelling, tasting and feeling.

And the most wonderful sixth sense: literally, to sense. We have all, at some point, sensed that someone was looking at us, or that something was about to happen, and then it did ...

Our sensing uses a combination of the other five senses and proprioception/spatial awareness. Some people have a stronger sixth sense than others, but it's actually something that can be practised!

To OBSERVE, is to be a watcher ...

A watcher of others, of surroundings AND of ourselves!

A teacher once told me that when I felt anxious or worried about something I should do this:

- see something with my eyes, 
- hear something with my ears, 
- and touch something with my hands or feet.

It works in that it takes us 'out' of our mind and brings us back to the here and now! Observation of any kind can bring us back to the present moment.

Did you know that our brains are wired for observational learning? That's why the saying goes 'Just watch and you'll learn.'

If we are blessed with eyesight, then from a young age we learn from watching. Now, certainly in our very early years, we learn from our family, friends, teachers etc.

However, at a certain point we 'grow up' and you may hear 'mind yourself' - literally meaning to keep yourself in mind.

It is accepted that we can be in charge of our physical and mental wellbeing, that we can at any point take notice and observe/watch ourselves.

BODMAS Practical Tools:

To observe gives us the nudge to be present in the moment. We can observe with any of our senses.

Maybe you'd like to start with something like this. When I was at school, we were taught to:

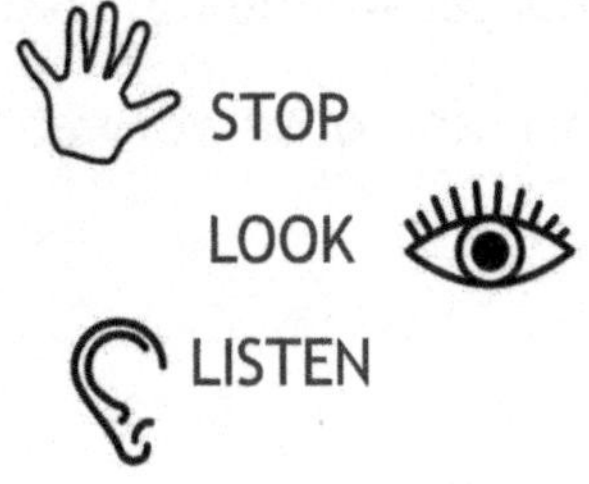

This was in the case of crossing the road and checking for cars, but perhaps we can use this tool to bring awareness to ourselves.

Take a moment to STOP, to LOOK at the situation in that moment, and then to LISTEN to what our needs are in that moment.

'To acquire knowledge, one must study; but to acquire wisdom, one must observe.'

Marilyn vos Savant

D.iscover

Definition: To find unexpectedly / to show interest in.

Discovery is a type of magic, I think.

That's not to say it's always good, and certainly it's not always a huge discovery either!

When we are little kids, a discovery like being able to go from sitting to standing is pretty huge and exciting. But maybe discovering you have forgotten about homework on a Sunday night isn't so much fun!

There is an art to discovery, I believe, and it is simple ... keep learning, keep playing, stay interested and inquisitive of the world and the people that are in it.

And that starts with you!

A good place to start practising discovery is to ask questions: why, where, how, who etc.

There isn't an end point to growing up. There isn't a button that we need to suddenly switch on to be a grown up, but interestingly maybe a button is switched off that we don't need (or want) to switch off. Our quest for discovery is what keeps us 'young at heart', as we grow older and wiser.

Observe the people around you without judgement, think about who you think is still discovering things and playing with life... Is their attitude to life different to those who maybe discover less?

Discovering can be just looking at things differently. Like ‘Ha yeh, I never thought of it that way.’ Or it can be the act of noticing something, like discovering a little cut on your finger you didn’t know was there... ‘Oh, hello little cut on my finger. Thanks body, for dealing with that!’

Good news is that there is no limit on discovery, it would be a boring world if there was eh?

BODMAS Practical Tools:

In this context, discovery will be about ourselves, our body, our feelings and our surroundings.

If in doubt, stop at...

If In...

I feel - I need

I feel tired - I need to rest.

I feel restless - I need to move.

I feel low, excited, emotional - I need a hug, a belly laugh, a cry.

Allowing ourselves the opportunity to rediscover ourselves every day is a wonderful and freeing way to live.

Whatever it is, discover like you are a small kid again, as if for the first time you are seeing how your fingers move and wriggle and pick things up, how scrunching up your nose feels.
Try it!

How you can balance on one leg without much work – be wowed by yourself!
You are constantly growing and changing and therefore YOU are the discovery!

You may be thinking.... Who me?

'You are under no obligation to be the person you were a year, month or even five minutes ago. You have the right to grow. No apologies.'

Alan Watts

M.OVE

Definition: The state of changing someone/something's position.

Now, moving ... that's a powerful force!

Have you ever felt a lot better after having a big old yawn or a good shake or dance? Well, that's not by accident!

Our bodies love to MOVE!

It is, after all, our moving machine.

These days, it has become common and acceptable to think of our movement as being at the gym or going for a jog... and yes, maybe they can be a part of our overall wellbeing.

However, movement is so much more than that.

Movement can be medicine for our body AND mind, in terms of how it can help transform our mood, physical health and overall relationship with our body. When we are small children we move instinctively.

We don't ask if spinning around till we're dizzy will be fun ... we just do it!

We make shapes with our body depending on our capabilities: we roll, climb, swing, jump, kick, hop and often fall a few times in between.

My wish for us all is that we continue into our adult years being playful. Our personal capabilities may be different, for sure, but I dare you to 'play more'. Move like you are watching your body, learning from your body rather than demanding of it.

I mentioned before that even a yawn can help with shaking things up.

Ever notice how cats and dogs do a huge stretch/yawn before they move too far after a nap? They are preparing their body and mind to move. In fact, most animals do the same, even a bird ruffles its feathers ... We seem to yawn less as we get older, but it's very natural and useful to us to maintain this tool.

There is a tendency as we 'grow up' that we leave behind a lot of our natural instincts.

I urge you, say NO!

I dare you to continue being playful, be silly ... put on a favourite tune in your room and just move. Try to listen to your body and what it might need from you in that moment, on that day, because no day is the same!

Even the smallest of movements can shift our mindset. The expression 'oh that's so moving', is a nod to our internal environment being affected by our external experience. So, remember, it doesn't have to be something grand.

Just start ... see where it goes!

Every time we consciously move our body, we are saying

'Hey there body, thanks. Love ya. x'

BODMAS Practical Tools:

How we move can say a lot about how we feel. That's one way we can pick up on how someone is feeling: we watch their body language. You can tell if someone is excited, sad, confident, nervous etc. by how they hold themselves. Let's say with pet animals, for example with a dog - if the dog is overexcited you can tell, and you can either be super excited with it in a high pitched voice and moving arms etc. or you can calm their energy down by speaking softly and calmly and maybe being very still.

Tuning in to how our body/mind feels is important.

Here are some ideas of how our movement can help us feel more connected.

Busy mind: tree pose

Sleepy/lazy: shaking/dancing

Struggling to concentrate: downward dog

These are certainly not the ONLY ways, but they are a good start and you will learn more about what you need the more you listen to yourself!!

'The fastest way to still the mind is to move the body.'

Gabrielle Roth

A.CCEPT

Definition: When a person recognises a situation or condition without attempting to change it or protest it.

Personally, I love the Latin translation of the word:

acquiescere - to find peace/rest in.

I think this is a beautiful description and a useful reminder to let things be and find peace in situations and people.

The phrase 'let it go' has long been used to help with situations that are out of our control.

As the Frozen character Elsa reminds us, yes, there are times where we can and should 'let it go'.

It takes practice and it is a very useful mantra. However, I have found over the years that 'let it BE' is much more realistic and rewarding.

Letting things be gives us permission to allow all that we're feeling to simply 'BE' there, and at the same time not have to 'do' anything.

Sometimes letting things 'go' takes effort. Instead, we see the 'things' and let them BE.

After all, the truest of self-love rituals should be that we don't torment ourselves with the 'what ifs' and 'if onlys' ...

We are not our thoughts!

I'll say that again ... we are not our thoughts. They are just visitors.

Just like our friend, the BREATH, our thoughts and feelings tell us things.

And, just like friends who give us advice or their opinion, sometimes we listen to them, sometimes we don't.

This is where meditation helps.

When we meditate, we are practising acceptance of all that is.

Our thoughts, our feelings, our situations. We learn how to 'be' with them, watch them as they come and go and not 'run away with our thoughts', as the expression goes.

The magic of acceptance is that, if we are sad, we can notice it as a visitor and know that it's okay to feel sad, and that it will pass.

The golden nugget here is that often it is more likely to pass quickly if we say: 'Oh, I'm feeling sadness right now,' and simply allow for some time to pass by, avoiding trying to 'fix it' or 'letting it go'.

If we 'let things go' too often, we may be letting a 'friend' by, without hearing the full message. Like saying 'I don't want to hear it' and rushing to move on.

The practice of acceptance will have HUGE benefits in our day-to-day experiences.

You'll find that maybe instead of getting upset at forgetting to do something, or someone being rude to you, you will think, 'Ah ok, this is happening.' You will learn to be truly in charge of yourself and your thoughts and experiences.

BODMAS Practical Tools:

Use the expression, 'No use crying over spilled milk.' The milk has spilled. All that is useful to us is what we do NOW.

I know, I know, it's easier said than done sometimes, right? Like if the milk spills on something important ... I guess this is the challenge itself. In this case taking action to clear it up to make sure no lasting stains remain will be part of the road to accepting. There is usually something that will help with the process of accepting – and sometimes it is 'doing' something.

The fact is that we are always in a better place to deal with things if we can accept that it happened in the first place.

Acceptance of the now.

A diagram that may help

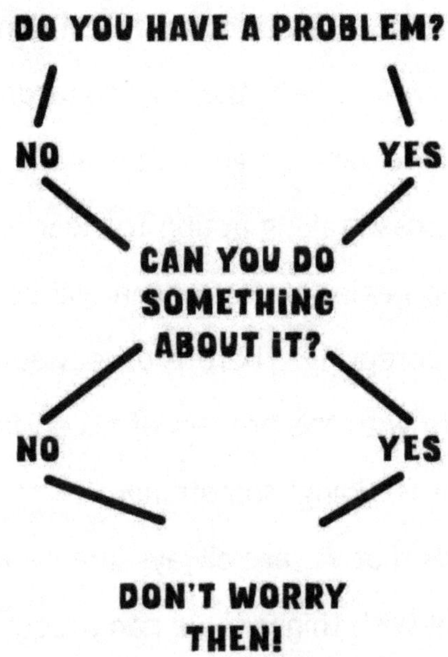

'Acceptance means:

For now, this is what this situation, this moment, requires me to do, and so I do it willingly.

Accept - then act. Whatever the present moment contains, accept it as if you had chosen it... this will miraculously transform your whole life.'

Eckhart Tolle

S.ilence

Definition: The absence of audible sound.

True audible silence is likely to be hard to find these days. It is seldom that we can determine fully the external environment when we want to invite silence in.

Silence is therefore an internal practice.

'The sound of silence' is one way to describe how to achieve quiet, peace, stillness. We may first benefit from listening IN.

It is obvious to note that when we are silent, we can still hear our breath, rumbles in our tummy, our heart beating and so on...

But listen more closely and we may just hear a deeper, more subtle sound: the sound of vibration, our internal body and the energy field that we are. Maybe a little like a gentle hum. Barely there, hardly noticeable and yet strangely recognisable and comforting.

If we practise silence, it can become the most powerful and transformative gifts we can give ourselves.
Truly like a hug from the universe whenever we need it.

(Related topic: Chapter – The Sound OM.)

BODMAS Practical Tools:

I'd like to think that this anagram was no coincidence

SILENT

LISTEN

Gift yourself some silent time

- to listen,
- to notice,
- to be.

For we are all stardust, cosmic beings in the form of humans. Getting familiar with our internal silence brings us clarity and presence in our external world.

You can try this:

Eyes closed, a vastness behind the eyelids (like opening your eyes, with your eyelids closed), lips lightly touching so you can breathe in and out through your nose, one hand on your heart, the other on your tummy.

- Breathe in slow.

- Breathe out deep.

  Repeat four to five times.

- Then breathe naturally

- Just be.

'There is a voice that doesn't use words.

Listen.'

Rumi

More Tips and Tools

The sound OM

The Big Bang Theory states that all matter emerged from a huge explosion.
In Yogic philosophies it is said that the universe was created from the sound of OM and that this 'sound' is ever present as it sustains us in our world.

If we are to understand that all matter vibrates, and that vibration holds sounds, then we can understand that we are sound itself.
Ever walk into a room and get a 'wrong vibe' or meet someone new and think 'they have a really cool vibe'? Similarly, we can all say we are intrinsically affected by music. It can change how we feel. It can resonate with us and really 'hit a chord'. A chord of our innate instrument. Our earthly vibration.

Cool fact:

OM has the vibrational frequency of 432 hertz. It is now known that the Earth's resonance is also 432 hertz.

It is in meditation and stillness that we may connect to this frequency of the universe.

The OM sound is broken into three separate sounds.

A - U - M.

We are encouraged to feel the sound of AUM reverberate through the body, starting from beneath the belly button and ending at the tip of our nose.

Find an audio of the sound OM, lie on your bed, close your eyes and listen...

tell me you don't feel at h**OM**e. :)

Chanting

Chanting is a tradition that originates in Indian religions called Kirtan.

Chanting is less about the words than it is about the vibration the words make when you say them. Sometimes a song can make us feel happy or sad without us necessarily knowing the words. There's a rhythm about the song, you may be singing the words, and they don't necessarily mean much to you, but the song is making you FEEL something.

Chanting is about creating a vibration. A tool we can use to bring awareness to ourselves. Some songs make us smile, some make us teary ... whatever needs to come up will do, if we let it!

If learning a new language is food for the brain, then chanting is food for the soul!

Mantra

Definition: A mantra can be a statement, phrase or a sound repeated frequently.

Why would we need that? Well, they can be helpful to remind us of lessons or messages that we need at certain times.

A little like reading a quote that really means something to you. You may find yourself remembering that quote and it helping you in certain situations in life.

Just think about when we learn to speak. To start with, the words are 'sounds' not 'meanings'; we attach meanings to the sound. For example, we learn that the sound 'ch-ai-r' means chair... Hehe, funny isn't it?

The chair is there whether we put a word/sound to it or not.

So in a way, mantras are sounds first, words second! The words used should make you feel something.

I'll give you an example of some mantras that I've leaned on through the years. Some have meaning, some just felt good. :)

- Trust the timing - This one has been my friend for a while, it really helps when I'm feeling nervous or anxious about a change that might be happening.
- I am nature - I use this one to help remind me that I am part of the earth, not just the human world.
- Ra Ma Da Sa OR Sa Ta Na Ma - these are Sanskrit Mantras which can be used in meditation.

Ra Ma Da Sa means: Sun, moon, earth, infinity. This Mantra supports healing and brings balance to our energetic being.

Sa Ta Na Ma means: Birth, life, death, rebirth. This comes from one of the oldest Mantras 'Sat Nam' meaning 'my true essence'

You can speak or chant these words or simply quietly in your mind, concentrate on the rhythm as you repeat the sounds in a loop. This is a technique used to hold our attention to our meditation and quieten the chatty mind.

Look up some versions of these (with or without music) and choose one that you really like.

Enjoy finding more mantras that become friends through life. Some will change along the way, and some will stick around!

Meditation

To try and summarise this vast topic, I will use an analogy I heard early in my meditation practice that helped enormously at the time and still does!
And to share the story I will start with a question ...

What does meditation do?

Well, picture an ocean, a vast sea that is always different, but always there. The surface is usually an indicator of what is going on with the weather or what's in the air or on the sea itself.
It can be smooth one minute then choppy the next. There can be a lot of goings on at the surface of the sea, and a lot of it isn't at the request of the ocean. Just below the surface there is a slightly different view. It's different because you can still possibly see the goings on above, but you are slightly separate to it, almost as though you are watching everything ... It may feel a little choppy but you're not getting involved.

Now, dive a little deeper down and we are entering a space in the sea where we can't see above the water, and we are now aware of the depth below. We perhaps observe a new world of fish swimming by 'without a care in the world'.

The thing is, crucially now we see that there is calm at the bed of the ocean, in spite of the goings on above.

Meditation helps us realise that we can be calm and settled like the bottom of the ocean, despite the noise or busyness of our surface/daily life, that anytime we feel that things are too much, or we can't cope, we can always find deep calm and quiet within ourselves.

That calm bed is inside us all.

'If the ocean can calm itself, then so can you.

We are both salt water mixed with air'

Nayyirah Waheed

As I pointed to in OBSERVE, sometimes we must

'Lose our mind, to come to our senses.'

Or, in other words, tell our mind to 'shhhhh!'

The MIND is our thinking machine. Therefore, meditation is NOT about 'not thinking' - it's more about watching/quietening our thoughts, or being separate to them.

It's like we are standing waiting for a train on the station platform, and our thoughts are the train carriages that pass by.

There are many trains that pass by, but we don't get on every carriage.

With meditation we learn to watch our thoughts pass by, like train carriages ... and we get to choose whether we get on the train or not.

It's so easy to jump on a 'train of thought' and we shouldn't think we've done anything wrong if we do. We simply accept that we did, and then jump off at the next station, as it were. The next station, of course, is exactly the moment you realise you jumped on the train in the first place - that's the magic!

A THOUGHT AND ANOTHER THOUGHT AND ANOTHER

As your meditation practice progresses, you will notice the time between each thought/carriage gets longer. But it is important to mention that every time we meditate will be different - so avoid going into a meditation thinking 'Right, let's see how long between carriages today?' It's not a competition with your mind haha.

Simply put in the time to meditate and see where it goes.

No expectation and no judgement!

How does that help in day-to-day life?

Well, if we accept that meditation allows us the pauses between thoughts, then we can accept that we can use that skill in daily life.

We will be able to put space between a thought and acting on it.

For example, if we get upset with someone after they say something rude, we have the ‘practice’ of taking a pause before we decide how we react.

Let me go back to the ocean story.

You see, after some practice of watching the waves of the ocean (watching your train of thoughts), you will find that the ocean has gifted you a surfboard, or a cool kayak, something you can use to 'ride the waves' smoothly and confidently in everyday life. Sure, sometimes we'll fall off or be challenged with a higher wave, but that's how we learn.

And guess what, that's how we grow.

I like to SEE with my eyes closed …

Think about it, long before we learn to meditate, we simply close our eyes and turn inwards.

Yes, sure, we can learn different techniques with help from tutors and courses etc., but remember, it starts here …

Close your eyes, breathe, be!

'Why do we close our eyes when we cry, pray, kiss and dream? Because some of the most beautiful things in life are not seen, but felt by the heart.' Denzel Washington

Worrying

We all worry, right?

Sometimes about small things, sometimes about big things.

Sometimes about things from the past and sometimes about things in the future.

Have you noticed, though, that we nearly never worry about the exact moment we are in?

Usually our worries are about things that are out of our control or things that haven't happened yet.

Our mind – our thinking machine – LOVES a story!

It can get so carried away with a story that it will trick you into thinking you have to 'solve' or spend time 'worrying' about things that are just 'part of the story'.

Gosh, sometimes it tells you the same story over and over again like a scene from a movie ...

Ever had that, when you have a scenario in your mind playing on repeat?

It can become a little tiring right?

Think of it this way...

The muscles you use for brushing your teeth have had a lot of practice over the years, right? Like, if you use the other arm it's a little sloppy and doesn't really feel comfortable ...

Now imagine brushing your teeth constantly for most of the day. Your arm would get tired. You're not meant to brush your teeth all day! :D

The mind may have had a lot of practice at story-telling and so it can become a habit to work all day on stories and scenarios that lead us to become ‘lost in our thoughts’.

Can you see how that could make us feel tired? After a whole day of brushing our teeth, we would definitely need to rest our arm, right?

Give it a chance to recharge and relax.

So, what helps us rest our mind?

Yeah, you got it ... Meditation! That’s the game changer!

The more we try and sit with our thoughts in silence and practise detachment from them - the more we can remember to pause the ‘mind story’ and come back to the present moment.

Mostly when we worry we are stuck in statements like ‘if only’ or ‘what if’, ‘I wish I did/didn’t’.

When we catch ourselves with this self-talk, a good little mantra that I say to myself is...

‘I am here now’ to pull me away from my worry chatter.

You could even use the **STOP LOOK LISTEN** technique here.

Also, a gentle reminder...

‘Not everything that weighs you down is yours to carry.’

‘Worrying doesn’t take away tomorrow’s trouble,

it takes away today’s peace.’

Unknown

: (: You Decide

Cool fact:

If you're feeling down, try this.

There has been research done that showed placing a pencil between our teeth, forcing our lips into a smile, can actually help us feel better. Strange, but it works! Remember that emotions come and go and sometimes we need something to trick our mind out of feeling blue.

By using the pencil to change our facial behaviour, it can affect our inner feelings and help lift us.

'Yesterday was heavy.
Put it down.'

Remember you deserve a good start to the day.

Breathing Practices

‘Sometimes the most important thing in a whole day is the rest we take between two deep breaths.’

Etty Hillesum

Box Breathing

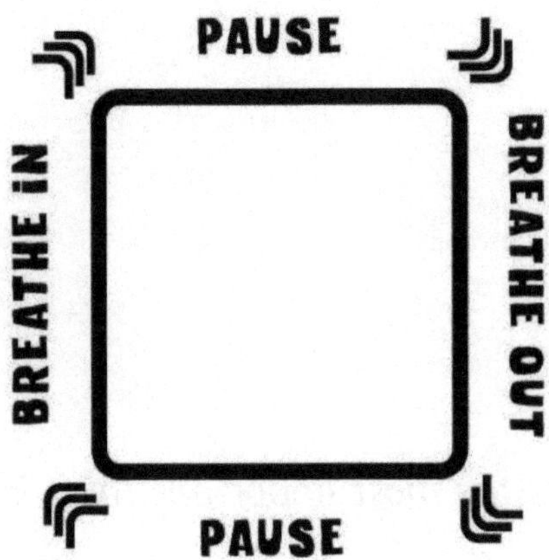

- Breathe in fully through your nose (fill the tummy) for four.
- Hold for four.
- Breathe out through your mouth (empty the tummy) for four.
- Hold for four.

Finger Tracing

- Stretch open one hand.
- With the other hand, using your index finger or a pencil,
- trace UP and DOWN each finger.
- Breathe IN as you trace UP a finger.
- Breathe OUT as you trace DOWN a finger.
- Go as slowly as you can and try to breathe in and out through your nose.

4 - 7 - 8 Breath Technique

Relaxing Breath, Dr Weil

This breath is one of my favourites - mainly because it involves numbers.

But it's also the one I use the most if I'm struggling to sleep or need a little relaxation/ winding down!

The basics are:

- Begin with a big audible exhale (like you are cooling down a hot bowl of soup).
- Breathe in through the nose for four counts.
- Hold your breath gently for seven counts.
- Breathe out through your mouth for eight counts.

This is one cycle.

Begin practising this breath sitting up tall and then when you are comfortable with it you can use it lying down to help with falling asleep or just relaxing!

Extra notes are:

- Breathe in quietly through your nose.
- When you breathe out through your mouth make a little whoosh sound.

It is recommended that you only repeat this cycle four times and if you'd like to get the most benefit from it repeat that twice each day.

Short Stories

I will share two very short stories that I have carried with me along my journey.

I hope you like them!

Ubuntu

Ubuntu is a Zulu or Xhosa word – an African concept that translates as: 'I am because we are.'

The story goes that an anthropologist was studying the culture and traditions of an African tribe for some time. On the day he was leaving, as he waited for his transportation, he decided to play a game with the village children. He had bought a big basket of sweets. He gathered the kids and told them to stand in a line and went to place the basket of sweets under a tree in the distance.

He said, 'When I say GO, the first one to the tree gets all the sweets.'

The kids looked super excited, and as he said 'GO' they unexpectedly all held hands and ran towards the tree together as a group. They joyously jumped and hugged and shared all the sweets.

In that moment the anthropologist understood the true essence of this community. He said to one little girl, 'Why did you all run together?'

She answered simply, 'How can one of us be happy if all others are sad? I am happy, because we are happy.'

Ubuntu!

Creation Story

Hopi Nation, Arizona

Creation said, 'I want to hide something from the humans. It is the realisation that they are the creator of their own reality.'

The Eagle said, 'Give it to me. I will take it to the moon.'

The Creator said, 'No, one day they will go to the Moon and find it there.'

The Salmon said, 'I will bury it at the bottom of the ocean.'

Creator said, ' No, they will go there too.'

The Buffalo offered, 'Let me take it and I'll bury it in the Great Plains.'

The Creator replied, 'They will cut into the skin of the earth and find it even there.'

Grandmother, who lives at the breast of Mother Earth and is blind but sees with spiritual eyes, said,

'Put it inside of them.'

The Creator answered, 'It is done.'

'It's the Heart that knows the path.

The mind is just there to organise the steps.'

Jeff Brown

Fill your cup / check your bucket

Some people use the expression 'fill your own cup first' or 'put your own oxygen mask on before helping others'. These expressions are a reminder that if we look after ourselves first then we are more likely to be able to help others too – and without it taking too much out of us.

In fact, we are able to be our best for others when we feel the best for ourselves.

Someone once described their busy life like they are constantly trying to fill a bucket with water but there is a hole in the bucket that they didn't know about and that was why it was never full.

The ultimate tools in self-care, are self-love and self-respect.

The least we can do for ourselves is to take the time to check that there isn't 'a hole in my bucket'.

I think, as an adult, it is so easy to get swept up with the 'doing' that we forget about just 'being' - after all we are human beings not human doings!

I'll share a little secret - adults want to be kids again!

Have you heard an adult you know say things like 'Look at them, without a care in the world,' or 'Oh to be carefree like that again'?

The truth is, our society is mostly gearing us up for 'growing up' and not for 'being here now'. Maybe what I want to get across to you is that being a grown up is not the end goal.

So it's not like, okay I'm an adult now ... now what?

I wish that this little box of tricks and stories can be the beginning of your adventure with YOU. The beginning of learning that the journey is the destination.

A destination to arrive HERE and NOW.

'But the beauty is in the walking -

we are betrayed by destinations.'

Gwyn Thomas

Everything that is important to you now and all the things you love, your dreams and wishes are still there when you 'grow up'.

Yes, of course, there has to be a little forward planning, but I would argue for a happy medium.

Maybe plan for the tomorrows but exist in the now's!

Look - here is a hard truth.

Being a teenager is sometimes hard. Being an adult is sometimes hard.

Guess what - life is sometimes hard!

BUT

Life is also sweeeeeeeeeeettttttt!

You know why? Because you're in it!

Yeah YOU!!!

I mean it. :)

Simple.

Go live.

Go shine.

Ride the waves of life.

Do BODMAS.

Fall.

Learn.

Apply.

Repeat.

Laugh.

Love.

Cry.

Ask for help.

Express.

Hug.

Sing.

Adventure.

Listen to stories.

Share stories.

Be silly.

Stumble.

Find courage.

Find gratitude.

Find compassion.

Find yourself.

Love yourself.

Love others.

Love this earth.

Love.

'The meaning of my existence is that life has addressed a question to me. Or, conversely, I myself am a question which is addressed to the world, and I must communicate my answer, for otherwise I am dependent upon the world's answer.'

Carl Jung

BODMAS SUMMARY

BREATHE:

Box breathing method, or any other technique you feel drawn to.

OBSERVE:

Stop. Look. Listen.

DISCOVER:

No matter how small or big, learn something new - notice yourself!
IF IN... I Feel, I Need...

MOVE:

Maybe you're on your own, so you dance and shake it off - or it may be that you simply yawn!
Listen + Mood = Movement

ACCEPT:

Give yourself permission to let it BE! Use the diagram if it helps.

SILENCE:

SILENT. LISTEN in to YOUR universe!

Now it's your turn...

What's your journey now?

Where would YOU like to go from here?

You may not know it yet or even for a long time...
But there is a story that the world needs to hear
and it's only YOU that can tell it!

Take your time. Enjoy the steps.
Don't be hard on yourself. You've got this.
I love you.

xx

'The journey of a thousand miles begins with a single step.'

Lao Tzu

What's your first step?

Thanks and Recommendations

My journey here and to this book has been made possible because those I have encountered on the road have been generous, kind and open with their own stories and wisdoms.

'I am one voice, but together we are a choir.'

Thank you especially to my girls for showing me the way.

Thank you to my guides and teachers for your bright lights and wisdoms.

To my family and community who hold me and support me and my dog Ziggy and his cuddles

Recommended books:

I'll keep this one easy ... ONE book I wish I'd read as a teenager:

The Four Agreements By Don Miguel Ruiz.

If you've read it already – YES! If not, go, go and buy it now!!! :)

LOVE,

Me x